Faster than fairies, faster than witches,
Bridges and houses, hedges and ditches;
And charging along like troops in a battle,
All through the meadows the horses and cattle:
All of the sights of the hill and the plain
Fly as thick as driving rain;
And ever again, in the wink of an eye,
Painted stations whistle by.

Here is a child who clambers and scrambles,
All by himself and gathering brambles;
Here is a tramp who stands and gazes;
And there is the green for stringing the daisies!
Here is a cart run away in the road
Lumping along with man and load;
And here is a mill and there is a river:
Each a glimpse and gone for ever!

VIKING

Published by the Penguin Group
Penguin Books USA Inc., 375 Hudson Street, New York, New York 10014, U.S.A.
Penguin Books Ltd, 27 Wrights Lane, London W8 5TZ, England
Penguin Books Australia Ltd, Ringwood, Victoria, Australia
Penguin Books Canada Ltd, 10 Alcorn Avenue, Toronto, Ontario,
Canada, M4V 3B2
Penguin Books (N.Z.) Ltd, 182–190 Wairau Road, Auckland 10, New Zealand

Penguin Books Ltd, Registered Offices: Harmondsworth, Middlesex, England

First published in Great Britain by Orion Children's Books, 1993
First published in the United States of America by Viking,
a division of Penguin Books USA Inc., 1993

1 3 5 7 9 10 8 6 4 2

Volume copyright © The Albion Press Ltd., 1993
Illustrations copyright © Llewellyn Thomas, 1993
All rights reserved

Library of Congress Catalog Card Number: 92–60037
ISBN 0-670-84894-8

Printed and bound in Singapore by Tien Wah Press (PTE) Ltd.
Set in Palatino

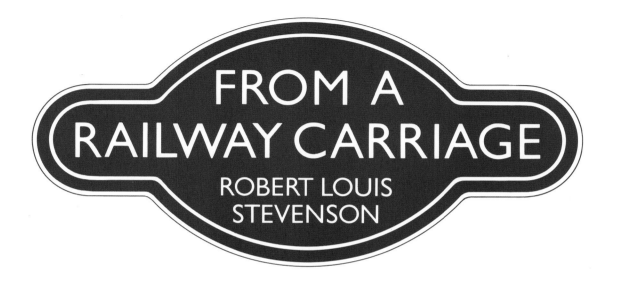

FROM A
RAILWAY CARRIAGE

ROBERT LOUIS STEVENSON

Illustrated by Llewellyn Thomas

VIKING

Faster than fairies,

faster than witches,

Bridges and houses,

hedges and ditches;

And charging along like troops in a battle,

All through the meadows the horses and cattle:

All of the sights of the hill and the plain
Fly as thick as driving rain;

And ever again, in the wink of an eye,

Painted stations whistle by.

Here is a child who clambers and scrambles,

All by himself and gathering brambles;

Here is a tramp who stands and gazes;

And there is the green for stringing the daisies!

Here is a cart run away in the road

Lumping along with man and load;

And here is a mill, and there is a river:

Each a glimpse and gone for ever!